anythink

D0691371

CAT
AND
DOG

For Maripaz, Harvey, and Ruby, who all
helped make this book. Thank you x

Copyright © 2019 by Jonathan Bentley

First published in Australia by Little Hare Books, an imprint of Hardie Grant Egmont.

All rights reserved. Published by Scholastic Press, an imprint of Scholastic Inc., *Publishers since 1920.*
SCHOLASTIC, SCHOLASTIC PRESS, and associated logos are trademarks and/or registered trademarks of Scholastic Inc.

The publisher does not have any control over and does not assume any responsibility for author or third-party websites or their content.

No part of this publication may be reproduced, stored in a retrieval system, or transmitted in any form or by any means, electronic, mechanical, photocopying, recording, or otherwise, without written permission of the publisher. For information regarding permission, write to Scholastic Inc., Attention: Permissions Department, 557 Broadway, New York, NY 10012.

This book is a work of fiction. Names, characters, places, and incidents are either the product of the author's imagination or are used fictitiously, and any resemblance to actual persons, living or dead, business establishments, events, or locales is entirely coincidental.

Library of Congress Cataloging-in-Publication Data available

ISBN 978-1-338-68470-4

10 9 8 7 6 5 4 3 2 1   21 22 23 24 25

Printed in the U.S.A. 40

First edition, March 2021

The text type was set in KG Ten Thousand Reasons Alt. The display type was set in Marujo.

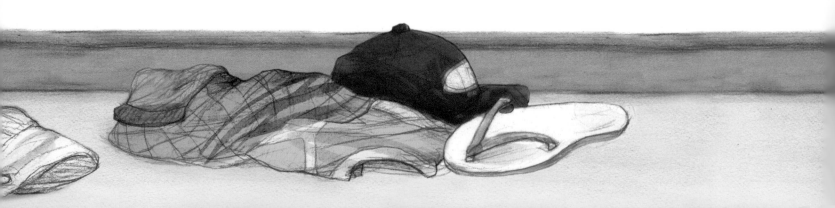

CAT AND DOG

JONATHAN BENTLEY

Scholastic Press • New York

A teeny tiny dog and a grumpy old kitty
were left home alone in a house near the city.

Would there be CHAOS and
MADNESS and MESS?

Or perfect behavior and peace (more or less)?

"CAT! CAT! CAT!"

barked Dog,

"We can't lounge around all day!

Let's escape to the park

so we can run and play!"

"But I'm a famous pet," sniffed Cat.

"An online celebrity.

If I play around outside,

someone's sure to recognize me."

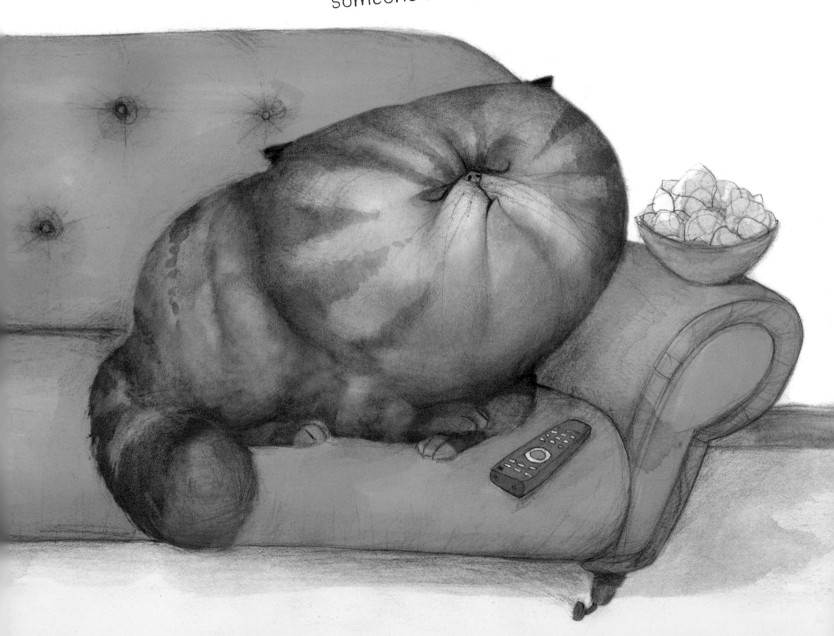

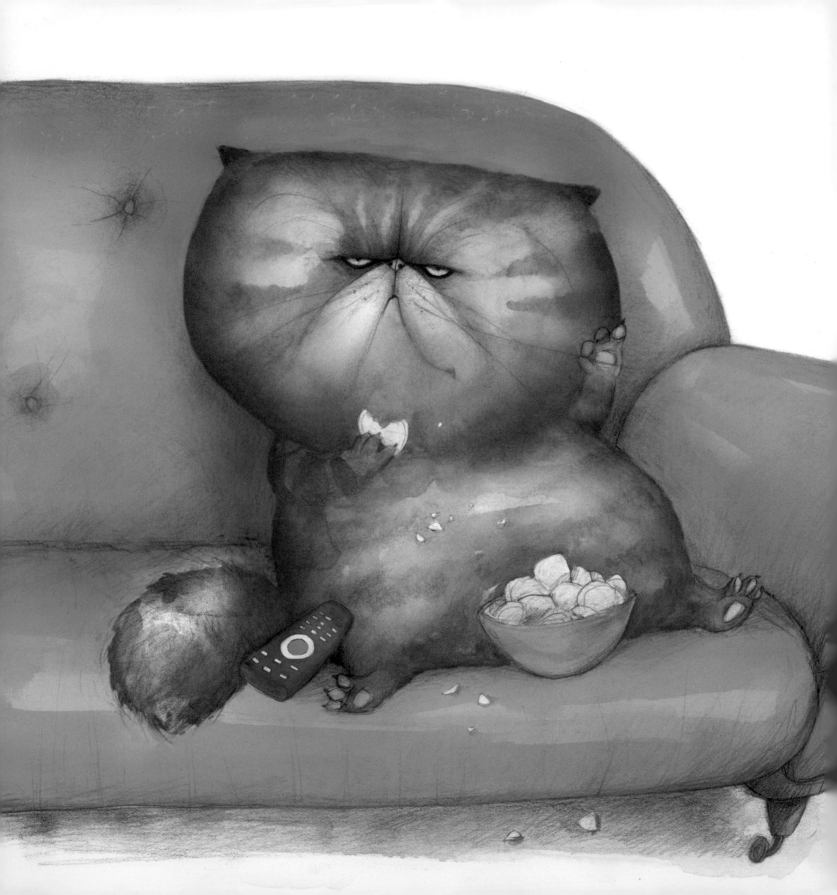

"Of course, Cat," said Dog, "you are handsome and wise. But if we dress up together, we could sneak out in disguise."

"How interesting," said Cat, with a very slight smile.

"This could be the moment to show off my style . . ."

Cat and Dog were very different,
but they agreed to play fair
as they searched for disguises
and **FABULOUS**
things to wear.

Hats, ribbons, and belts

were all part of the game,

as Dog thought of freedom

and Cat thought of fame.

Oh, what **fun** the pair had!

They made a

HUGE,
UGLY MESS . . .

But they were being creative,

so they couldn't care less.

They cut and they glued,

they hammered and painted –

they worked with such speed

that poor Cat nearly fainted!

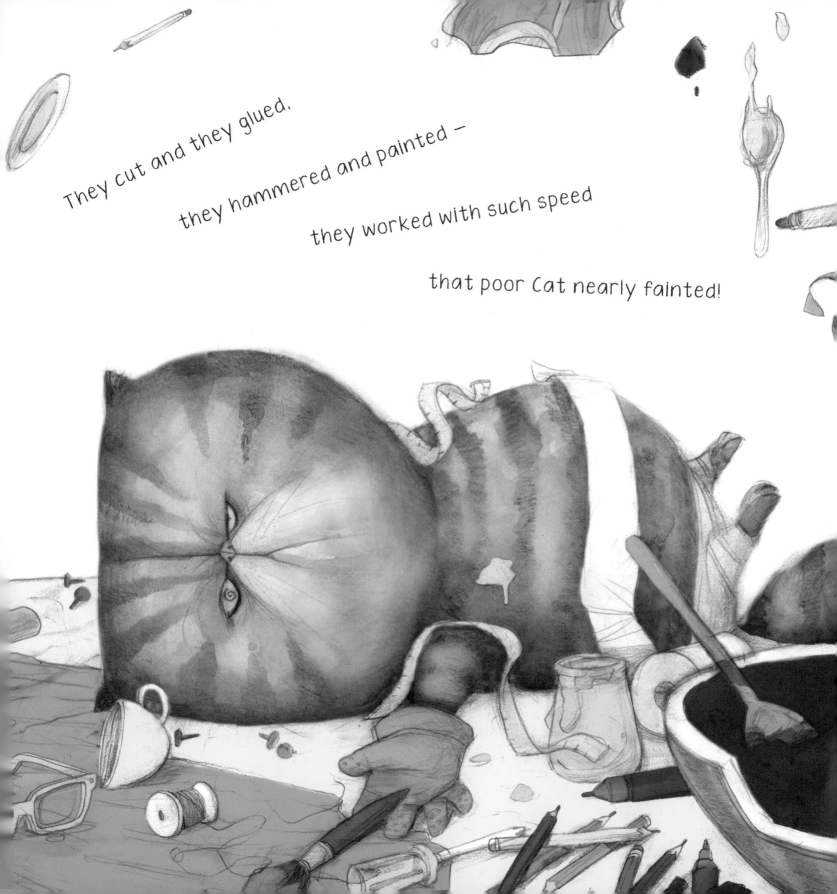

After a snack, THEY WERE BACK!

With a flourish, out came Cat,

dazzling in his cape and his watermelon hat.

"I know I look magnificent,"
said Cat with a fancy twirl.
"I'm ready to hit the town —
let's give this thing a whirl!"

DOG BOUNDED

out next, in her own cape and mask.
If adventure was the game, she was ready for the task.

"I'm with you, Cat," said Dog.
"Together our plan can't fail."
Then she struck a playful pose
and excitedly wagged her tail.

It was time to sneak out of the door —

the final step in the great escape plan,

but then Cat tripped on Dog's cape,

tumbled forward . . . and turned on the fan.

And that is when things got

COMPLETELY

OUT OF

HAND...

And just when you were thinking
things were as bad as they could be,

Cat and Dog's family arrived home
with a click and turn of the key.

Our friends had to move quickly!
They made a last-minute dash —
coming to each other's rescue
and tidying the house in a flash.

IT WAS A **MIRACLE!**
They'd done it —
they'd put all their mess away.

But their daring plan
for escape
would have to wait for
another day.